D1451002

UNCOVERING
AMERICAN HISTORY™

A PRIMARY SOURCE INVESTIGATION OF

WOMEN'S SUFFRAGE

MEREDITH DAY AND COLLEEN ADAMS

rosen publishing's
rosen
central

Published in 2016 by The Rosen Publishing Group, Inc.
29 East 21st Street, New York, NY 10010

Library of Congress Cataloging-in-Publication Data

Day, Meredith.
A primary source investigation of women's suffrage/Meredith Day and
Colleen Adams.
     pages cm.—(Uncovering American history)
Includes bibliographical references and index.
ISBN 978-1-4994-3519-1 (library bound)
1. Women—Suffrage—United States—History—Juvenile literature. 2.
Women—Suffrage—United States—History–Sources—Juvenile literature.
3. Suffragists—United States—History—Juvenile literature. I. Adams,
Colleen. II. Title.
JK1898.D39 2016
324.6'230973—dc23

                                                                    2014044173

Manufactured in the United States of America

CONTENTS

Voting is one of the most important rights for citizens in a democracy. Throughout history, countries have limited the right to vote, which is also known as suffrage. In the past in the United States, only white men who owned property were allowed to voice their opinions about the government by voting. The idea that all citizens—regardless of gender, race, or wealth—should have the vote is relatively recent.

One of the most famous early supporters of women's rights was Abigail Adams. Her husband, John Adams, later became the second president of the United States. In 1787, he was a delegate to the Second Continental Congress, which drafted the United States Constitution. The Constitution stated that "all men are created equal." Abigail Adams noticed a problem with that statement. She wrote to John:

I desire you would remember the Ladies, and be more generous and favorable to them than your ancestors. Do not put such unlimited power into the hands of

Equal Franchise Society

Legislative Series

(EXTRACT FROM A LETTER FROM MRS. ABIGAIL ADAMS TO HER HUSBAND JOHN ADAMS)

"I long to hear that you have declared our independency. And, by the way, in the new code of laws which I suppose it will be necessary for you to make, I desire you would remember the ladies and be more generous and favorable to them than your ancestors. Do not put such unlimited power into the hands of the husbands. Remember, all men would be tyrants if they could. If particular care and attention is not paid to the ladies, we are determined to foment a rebellion, and will not hold ourselves bound by any laws in which we have no voice or representation.

"That your sex are naturally tyrannical is a truth so thoroughly established as to admit of no dispute; but such of you as wish to be happy willingly give up the harsh title of master for the more tender and endearing one of friend. Why, then, not put it out of the power of the vicious and the lawless to use us with cruelty and indignity with impunity?

— "Braintree, March 31, 1776"

In the early twentieth century, the Equal Franchise Society distributed fliers with quotes supporting women's rights, such as Abigail Adams's famous "Remember the Ladies" letter.

the Husbands, remember all Men would be tyrants if they could. If particular care and attention is not paid to the Ladies we are determined to foment a Rebellion, and will not hold ourselves bound by any Laws in which we have no voice, or Representation.

Abigail Adams believed that it was dangerous to give all the power in a new government to men. But that was what happened in the U.S. Constitution. In addition to being unable to vote, women in early American history were often not allowed to own property, get a divorce, serve on juries, or speak in public.

As time went on, more people shared the view that women should have equal rights. Abraham Lincoln, a young lawyer in Illinois and another future president, wrote a letter to the *Sangamon Journal* in 1836. He said that all white people should have the right to vote as long as they were willing to carry the responsibilities of making decisions for the government of the United States. These responsibilities included paying taxes and going to war. Lincoln also added that this "right of suffrage" should not exclude females.

Still, in the early nineteenth century, women in the United States could not vote. Early on, a few colonies had allowed women to vote if they owned a certain amount of property. New Jersey was the last place to take away women's suffrage, in 1807. After that, sixty-two years went by before women gained the right to vote anywhere else in the nation. Women's suffrage did not become national law until 1920. That important victory occurred after decades of hard work by suffragists, who believed that women should be considered equal to men under the law.

★ CHAPTER ONE

ABOLITIONISM AND WOMEN'S RIGHTS

This engraving shows Lucretia Mott escaping a proslavery mob.

T he women's suffrage movement was greatly inspired by the abolitionist movement in the early 1800s. Abolitionists were people who fought to abolish, or end, slavery. They believed that blacks should be free and have the same rights as whites.

One of the best known abolitionists was William Lloyd Garrison. He believed in equal rights for everyone: black and white, male and female. In 1833, he founded the American Anti-Slavery Society.

Lucretia Mott, a Quaker minister and abolitionist, became a member of

QUAKERS

Quakers are members of the Religious Society of Friends, which is a denomination of Christianity. The religious movement was founded in England in the mid-1600s. Many Quakers immigrated in the 1700s to Britain's North American colonies, especially Pennsylvania.

Unlike at most churches, a clergyman does not lead the Quakers in worship. Instead, all members are encouraged to speak at meetings, even the women. Those who are particularly good public speakers are recognized as ministers. Lucretia Mott became a Quaker minister in 1821. Her experience as a minister helped her be comfortable speaking out about abolition and women's rights.

Quakers were also known for being opposed to war and slavery. However, not all of them were abolitionists, as Mott was. Angelina and Sarah Grimké had to leave their Quaker community in Philadelphia because some male members thought their antislavery activities were too controversial.

Garrison's group and cofounded the Philadelphia Female Anti-Slavery Society the same year. Garrison and Mott believed it was important for women to have equal rights: to be educated, hold a job, own property, and have custody of their children. These basic rights were similar to the rights that the abolitionists fought to gain for slaves.

Although the American Anti-Slavery Society was initially run by men, women soon took major roles in the

SARAH AND ANGELINA GRIMKÉ

Sarah and Angelina Grimké were sisters from Charleston, South Carolina, who became well-known abolitionists. Their father, John Faucheraud Grimké, was an attorney and plantation owner who had many slaves. Unlike the Grimkés, most abolitionists lived in the North and had never actually seen how slaves were treated. By sharing their firsthand experience of the evils of slavery, the Grimké sisters provided a new perspective to the abolitionist movement.

Sarah moved to Philadelphia in 1821, and Angelina joined her eight years later. Both of them converted to Quakerism because its members were against slavery. In 1835, Angelina wrote a letter to William Lloyd Garrison, who published it in his newspaper, the *Liberator*. Soon, Angelina and Sarah Grimké became public speakers for Garrison's American Anti-Slavery Society. They

(*continued on the next page*)

Angelina Grimké was a prominent opponent of slavery in the 1830s. At that time, not many women or people from the South were speaking out about equal rights.

(continued from the previous page)

were the first women to be public agents for the antislavery cause. At their "parlor meetings," they addressed both men and women, which was unheard of at the time.

In 1838, Angelina married Theodore Weld, a fellow abolitionist. The sisters continued to speak publicly and write appeals about both the abolition of slavery and the rights of women. Though they faced a lot of criticism for their actions during their lives, they are now recognized as pioneers of the women's rights movement.

movement. They had opportunities to speak and write about their objections to slavery and to take an active role in a political organization.

THE WORLD ANTI-SLAVERY CONVENTION

In 1840, Lucretia Mott and other women from the American Anti-Slavery Society were chosen to attend the World Anti-Slavery Convention in London, England, with the male delegates. When they arrived, the British abolitionists voted to exclude the women. Women were asked to sit in the gallery and observe the events, but they were not allowed to participate.

William Lloyd Garrison sat with the women in protest of their exclusion and argued on their behalf. He believed that women should share equal roles as speakers and officers of the organization. Another American abolitionist

William Lloyd Garrison's abolitionist newspaper, the *Liberator*, was first published on January 1, 1831. The last issue came out on December 29, 1865, just a few weeks after slavery was abolished.

who loudly supported the women was Wendell Phillips. He went on to become a well-known public speaker in favor of both abolitionism and women's rights. Even some British men opposed the decision to exclude women. Daniel O'Connell, a member of Parliament, and writer William Howitt wrote letters to Lucretia Mott offering their support. Mott was determined to make a difference as an abolitionist and supporter of women's rights issues. Her gentle manner of dealing with people later helped her become a key figure in the establishment and organization of the women's rights movement.

At the World Anti-Slavery Convention, Mott met Elizabeth Cady Stanton, who would also become one of the most influential leaders of the women's movement. Stanton was in London on her honeymoon. She was already developing her radical ideas about women's equality with men. When she married her husband, Henry Brewster Stanton, she had refused to say in her vows that she would obey him.

After Mott and Stanton were denied the right to participate in the antislavery convention, they started thinking. They spent the rest of their time brainstorming ideas for another convention: one that would fight for women's rights.

WOMEN'S RIGHTS IN THE 1840S

Although the first women's convention did not take place until eight years after Stanton and Mott first discussed it, they both worked for causes related to women's rights from 1840 to 1848. Mott became more active in the women's antislavery society and continued to write and speak about equal rights for women. Stanton gave public speeches and spoke to members of the New York legislature. She hoped to change the law to allow married women to own their own property and keep their own earnings in New York State. Her efforts paid off: in April 1848, New York passed the Married Women's Property Act, which was updated to give them even more rights in 1860.

Historians believe that Mott and Stanton were greatly influenced by the traditions of the Iroquois Nation in upstate New York. Iroquois women generally enjoyed more equality with their husbands than white women did. They were trusted to nominate the male chiefs who would represent their clan at the Iroquois Grand Council. In the summer of 1848, Mott visited the Seneca nation of the Iroquois. They were in the midst of meetings to change their governmental structure, and women were equal partners to the men in this process. Mott was inspired to see the Iroquois women participate in their nation's government. It gave her hope that all American women would someday earn the same respect from the United States government. That same summer, Mott and Stanton finally put their plans for a women's rights convention into action.

WOMAN SUFFRAGE

★ CHAPTER TWO

THE SENECA FALLS CONVENTION

T he first women's rights convention took place in Seneca Falls, New York, on July 19 and 20, 1848. This was when the women's rights movement really took off, especially the campaign for women's suffrage. In addition to Lucretia Mott and Elizabeth Cady Stanton, other women participated in the planning of the convention. Most of them were Quakers, like Mott.

THE DECLARATION OF SENTIMENTS

The organizers of the convention held several meetings in the summer of 1848 to plan their event. Although Mott lived in Philadelphia, she visited upstate New York often and participated in the planning. One of the most important meetings took place on July 16, 1848, at Mary Ann M'Clintock's home in Waterloo, New York. Also present at the meeting were Stanton, Mott, Mott's sister Martha Wright, and Jane Hunt. In McClintock's parlor, the group began to draft a formal statement to be presented at the convention. Stanton did the majority of the writing of the statement, which was titled the Declaration of Sentiments. It outlined the basic premise for the convention: equal rights for women, including the right to vote.

The Declaration of Sentiments modeled the same structure as the Declaration of Independence. In fact, Stanton mimicked the exact language used in the preamble of the Declaration of Independence of 1776. But she made a crucial addition. The Declaration of Independence had said that "all men are created equal" and have the right to "life, liberty, and the pursuit of happiness." Now women demanded their inclusion: "all men and women are created equal."

The Declaration of Sentiments then listed eighteen grievances, or complaints, to explain the ways

THE FIRST CONVENTION

EVER CALLED TO DISCUSS THE

Civil and Political Rights of Women,

SENECA FALLS, N. Y., JULY 19, 20, 1848.

———

WOMAN'S RIGHTS CONVENTION.

———

A Convention to discuss the social, civil, and religious condition and rights of woman will be held in the Wesleyan Chapel, at Seneca Falls, N. Y., on Wednesday and Thursday, the 19th and 20th of July current; commencing at 10 o'clock A. M. During the first day the meeting will be exclusively for women, who are earnestly invited to attend. The public generally are invited to be present on the second day, when Lucretia Mott, of Philadelphia, and other ladies and gentlemen, will address the Convention.*

———

* This call was published in the *Seneca County Courier*, July 14, 1848, without any signatures. The movers of this Convention, who drafted the call, the declaration and resolutions were Elizabeth Cady Stanton, Lucretia Mott, Martha C. Wright, Mary Ann McClintock, and Jane C. Hunt.

In the week before the first women's rights convention, the organizers advertised for it in local papers and prepared the Declaration of Sentiments.

THE M'CLINTOCK HOUSE

The M'Clintock House, originally located in Waterloo, New York, was the house of Thomas and Mary Ann M'Clintock, who came to the area in 1836 from Pennsylvania. As members of the Waterloo Quaker community, the M'Clintocks became active in the abolition and women's rights movements. The M'Clintock family lived in the two-story brick house for twenty years before returning to Pennsylvania.

The Woman's Rights National Historic Park in Seneca Falls, New York, bought the M'Clintock House in 1985. The house was moved to Seneca Falls with other famous historic sites of the women's rights movement, such as the home of Elizabeth Cady Stanton and the Wesleyan Chapel.

The M'Clintocks also opened their home to runaway slaves on the Underground Railroad. Visitors can tour the house and learn about its role in abolitionism and women's rights.

that men treated women as inferior. A woman had to obey the law, even though she had no voice in the government. She also could not attend college, own property, or participate publicly in most churches. In every aspect of life, men "endeavored . . . to destroy her confidence in her own powers." In other words, women often felt helpless because men did not treat them equally.

The Declaration of Sentiments also stated that women should have the right to vote. At first, even Mott was worried about that. She told Stanton that it would make them sound "ridiculous." But Stanton insisted that suffrage had to be included. The Seneca Falls women knew that not everyone would agree with their opinions. Yet they were still prepared to fight for equal human rights, even if they would be criticized or mocked.

AT THE CONVENTION

The organizers advertised for the convention. One announcement was published in the *Seneca County Courier* on July 14, 1848, five days before the convention. It invited only women to attend on the first day and asked the general public to attend on the second day to hear Lucretia Mott address the convention.

Elizabeth Cady Stanton read the Declaration of Sentiments on the first day, July 19. In the afternoon, another important document, the Declaration of Resolutions, was read. It outlined eleven specific rights that women ought to have. The Declaration of Sentiments had blamed men for treating women unfairly. But the leaders of the convention believed that women had to take responsibility for their own rights, too. The Declaration of Resolutions encouraged women to insist on equal treatment. It said that "it is the duty of the women of this country" to fight for suffrage and free speech. Since women and men have "the same capabilities," women should demand to be treated as men's equal in the community.

Over three hundred people came to the convention. At least forty of those in attendance were men. Frederick Douglass, an abolitionist and former slave, spoke in support of all the resolutions, including the one that most people resisted, giving women the right to vote. He stated that without it, women would have no way to protect their rights or make changes in the laws. After much discussion and debate, the resolution on women's suffrage finally passed. By the end of the convention, sixty-eight women and thirty-two men had signed the declaration.

REACTION TO THE CONVENTION

Some newspapers, especially in the area near Seneca Falls, praised the convention. The *North Star* in Rochester, New York, agreed that all "members of the human family" should be equal. Its editors applauded the convention's leaders for their "brilliant talents."

However, many people did not approve of the convention. Negative reactions were expressed all over the country by the press and some members of the clergy. Even other newspapers in upstate New York were opposed to women's rights. The *Recorder* in Syracuse called the women's movement "excessively silly," while the *Mechanic's Advocate* in Albany said it was "all wrong" and "unwomanly." Many of the people who had signed the declaration withdrew their names and support. Only the antislavery newspapers continued to write articles in favor of women's rights.

But the activists who had organized the Seneca Falls Convention did not let the naysayers stop them from fighting

SOJOURNER TRUTH

Sojourner Truth, a former slave, gained her freedom in 1827. She joined the abolitionist movement and traveled throughout the United States speaking out against slavery and supporting women's rights. Her speeches inspired many people to fight for universal suffrage for blacks and women.

Truth listened quietly to speakers at an Ohio women's rights convention in 1851. Some people made negative comments about women, expressing the opinion that they may not be as smart as men. In response, Truth gave a fiery and memorable speech that later came to be known as "Ain't I a Woman?" She argued that because she had suffered the same hardships as men, she deserved the same rights.

Born Isabella Baumfree, Sojourner Truth changed her name and began speaking out about slavery in 1843.

for their rights. Local women's rights conventions were held in several states. Throughout the 1850s, a National Women's Rights Convention was held almost every year.

William Lloyd Garrison was the vice president of the National Women's Rights Convention in Cleveland in 1853. He gave a speech expressing his strong opinions about women's rights. He defended the right of women to share in the decision-making processes with men in all levels of local, state, and national government. Although many people thought that Garrison's views on abolition and women's rights were too radical for the time, he continued to fight for justice and equal rights throughout his life.

LEADING THE MOVEMENT

Prominent leaders of the women's rights movement emerged by the mid-1850s. Lucy Stone and Susan B. Anthony had not attended the Seneca Falls Convention, but they, along with Stanton, were the most important women's rights activists of the next half-century. Stone graduated from Oberlin College in Ohio, the first college in the United States to admit women and African Americans. Unlike almost all women in the nineteenth century, she did not change her name when she married Henry Browne Blackwell. Anthony grew up in a Quaker family that believed in social reform. Her parents and sister attended the Seneca Falls Convention. She first became interested in women's rights when she was paid less than the male teachers at her school.

Each of these three leaders had different strengths. Stone was a brilliant public speaker who made audiences believe in what she had to say. Stanton was more persuasive in writing. She produced many speeches, petitions, and articles to get the word out about women's rights. Anthony's strengths were her drive and

Susan B. Anthony (*left*) and Elizabeth Cady Stanton, shown here in the 1880s, were friends and fellow activists for over fifty years.

organizational skills. She traveled extensively around the country, delivering speeches that were often written by Stanton. Together, these women and many others like them devoted much of their time and effort to gain more attention and support for women's rights.

CHAPTER THREE

SUFFRAGE IN THE RECONSTRUCTION ERA

I n 1851, Stanton and Anthony met for the first time and began their fifty-year partnership working for women's rights and suffrage. In 1852, they started an organization called the New York Women's Temperance Society. Temperance, which means not drinking alcohol, was another popular social reform during this time period. Many women believed that drinking too much alcohol was dangerous to society, and they got involved in the temperance movement. Stanton believed that drunkenness was so dangerous that women should be allowed to divorce their husbands if they drank too much. In the nineteenth century, most people were opposed to divorce. Even when divorce was allowed, it was often much easier for a man to leave his marriage than for a woman to do the same.

Many suffragists continued to support the abolition of slavery in addition to women's suffrage. After the Civil War, they were hopeful that both African Americans and women would gain new rights. This period was known as Reconstruction because laws were passed to help the North and the South reunite. Many of these laws were meant to give rights to former slaves. However, Reconstruction did not lead to women's suffrage.

THE THIRTEENTH AMENDMENT

When the Civil War broke out in 1861, women put their efforts into winning the war and abolishing slavery. Many women ran their homes or businesses alone and became more independent while the men were away at war. They devoted their time to the war effort and put any further political action for women's rights on hold.

Even before the war ended in April 1865, both the House and the Senate had passed the Thirteenth Amendment to the U.S. Constitution, which abolished slavery. In order for it to become law, three-fourths of the states had to ratify, or approve, the amendment. After the war, Congress declared that Southern states would have to abolish slavery before their representatives could rejoin Congress. Many states in both the North and the South quickly

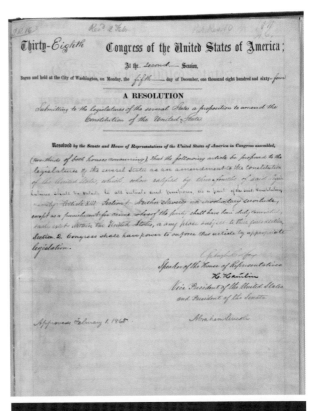

Congress proposed the Thirteenth Amendment in a joint resolution on December 5, 1864. President Abraham Lincoln signed it on February 1, 1865, sending it to the states for ratification.

ratified the Thirteenth Amendment, and it became law on December 6, 1865.

THE FOURTEENTH AMENDMENT

However, abolitionists were not done fighting just because slaves were free. They also wanted to ensure that former slaves would have the same rights as white Americans. The American Equal Rights Association was founded in 1866 by Susan B. Anthony, Elizabeth Cady Stanton, Lucretia Mott, and Lucy Stone. Mott headed the organization, which merged suffragists with members of the American Anti-Slavery Association. With so much focus on ensuring equality between races, suffragists were optimistic that women would gain equal rights, too.

Next, in 1866, Congress passed the Fourteenth Amendment. The purpose of the Fourteenth Amendment was to protect African Americans and guarantee them rights as citizens of the United States. It also said that if a state did not allow all male adult citizens to vote, some of that state's representatives in Congress would be taken away. This was a problem for the women's rights movement. It was the first time that the Constitution had used the word "male" to refer to voters. This caused disagreements between abolitionists and women's rights activists. Strong women's rights supporters like Stanton and Anthony did not support the Fourteenth Amendment because it essentially said only men, not women, had the right to vote.

Stanton, Anthony, and Stone sent out a petition asking women to write to Congress to protest the amendment because it excluded women. Regardless, the Fourteenth Amendment was ratified in 1868.

A PETITION

FOR

UNIVERSAL SUFFRAGE.

‧ ‧ ‧

To the Senate and House of Representatives:

The undersigned, Women of the United States, respectfully ask an amendment of the Constitution that shall prohibit the several States from disfranchising any of their citizens on the ground of sex.

In making our demand for Suffrage, we would call your attention to the fact that we represent fifteen million people—one half the entire population of the country—intelligent, virtuous, native-born American citizens; and yet stand outside the pale of political recognition.

The Constitution classes us as "free people," and counts us *whole* persons in the basis of representation; and yet are we governed without our consent, compelled to pay taxes without appeal, and punished for violations of law without choice of judge or juror.

The experience of all ages, the Declarations of the Fathers, the Statute Laws of our own day, and the fearful revolution through which we have just passed, all prove the uncertain tenure of life, liberty and property so long as the ballot—the only weapon of self-protection—is not in the hand of every citizen.

Therefore, as you are now amending the Constitution, and, in harmony with advancing civilization, placing new safeguards round the individual rights of four millions of emancipated slaves, we ask that you extend the right of Suffrage to Woman—the only remaining class of disfranchised citizens—and thus fulfil your Constitutional obligation "to Guarantee to every State in the Union a Republican form of Government."

As all partial application of Republican principles must ever breed a complicated legislation as well as a discontented people, we would pray your Honorable Body, in order to simplify the machinery of government and ensure domestic tranquillity, that you legislate hereafter for persons, citizens, tax-payers, and not for class or caste.

For justice and equality your petitioners will ever pray.

NAMES.	RESIDENCE.
Elizabeth Stanton	New York
Susan B. Anthony	Rochester – N.Y.
Antoinette Brown Blackwell	New York
Lucy Stone	Newark N. Jersey
Joanna S. Morse	48 Livingston. Brooklyn
Ernestine L. Rose	New York
Harriet E. Eaton	6. West 14th Street N.Y.
Catharine C. Wilkeson	83 Clinton Place New York
Elizabeth R. Tilton	48 Livingston St. Brooklyn
Mary Fowler Gilbert	295 W. 19th St New York
Mary E. Gilbert	New York
M. Griffith	New York.

Women's rights activists, including Stanton, Anthony, and Stone, sent this petition to Congress asking for the right to vote. (For a transcription, please see page 50–51).

THE FIFTEENTH AMENDMENT

The Thirteenth and Fourteenth Amendments had given former slaves many rights. The last step was to ensure

SUFFRAGE IN KANSAS

In 1867, there was a referendum in Kansas to decide whether to enfranchise more people. Current voters faced two questions: granting suffrage to black men and granting suffrage to women. The American Equal Rights Association (AERA) was eager to pass both proposals. But campaigning for the two causes proved difficult. Most of the AERA leaders did not have enough money to go out to Kansas and rally voters. That made it hard for them to promote equal rights and encourage people to vote yes on both questions. Instead, local politicians dominated the race. Most of them did not want either women or black men to gain the vote.

The result was very disappointing for the AERA, as the white male voters in Kansas defeated both black suffrage and women's suffrage. From this setback, the women's rights activists learned that securing their rights would be much harder than they thought. They began to argue about the direction of their movement. Lucy Stone disagreed with some of the tactics Susan B. Anthony and Elizabeth Cady Stanton had tried to use in Kansas. Eventually, in 1869, the AERA broke up into two women's suffrage groups, one led by Stone and one led by Anthony and Stanton.

their suffrage with one more constitutional change, the Fifteenth Amendment. But the conflict between abolitionists and women's rights activists worsened.

Abolitionist Wendell Phillips had long supported women's rights. But he now believed that women would have to wait their turn to vote. In a speech at the American Anti-Slavery Society's annual meeting on May 13, 1865, he had said, "This is the negro's hour." Many abolitionists agreed with him, even other allies of the women's rights movement like William Lloyd Garrison and Frederick Douglass. They felt it was most important for black men to be given the same rights as other men. They wanted to focus on black male suffrage first, rather than worrying about women's suffrage at the same time. "The negro's hour" became a kind of rallying cry for black male suffrage. Stanton and Anthony

Wendell Phillips supported the Fifteenth Amendment even though it gave the vote only to black men, leaving women of all races still disenfranchised.

were offended. They had worked just as hard as anyone else to secure rights for African Americans. They believed that now was the time to enfranchise Americans of all races and genders.

In 1869, the suffrage movement split into two groups over these disagreements. Stanton and Anthony founded the National Woman Suffrage Association (NWSA), dedicated to fighting for women's suffrage. It was based in New York. Stone headed the Boston-based American Woman Suffrage Association (AWSA). Its members still believed in women's suffrage, but they were willing to give black men the right to vote first.

Stanton and Anthony, who had fought so long and hard for equal rights for both women and blacks, insisted that women's suffrage should be included in the Fifteenth Amendment. The Fifteenth Amendment, which was ratified in 1870, stated that citizens of the United States could not be denied the right to vote based on "race, color, or previous condition of servitude." African Americans were officially allowed to vote. But the amendment did not say anything about gender. That meant women, in all likelihood, would continue to be denied the right to vote.

The Thirteenth and Fourteenth Amendments had freed the slaves and granted them the same rights as white Americans. Yet it had only given those rights to black men. Women, black and white alike, still did not have a voice in government.

CHAPTER FOUR

A DIVIDED MOVEMENT

The women's rights movement remained divided into two separate organizations, the NWSA and the AWSA, for twenty-one years. During that time, women slowly began to gain the right to vote in some local elections. Susan B. Anthony and Elizabeth Cady Stanton, of the NWSA, continued writing about their ideas, giving speeches, and organizing the women's movement. But just as Stanton and Anthony had feared, universal black male suffrage was not quickly followed by universal women's suffrage.

THE REVOLUTION

The *Revolution*, a weekly women's rights newspaper first published in Rochester, served as the platform for the NWSA. It discussed issues such as divorce and discrimination against women in the workplace. Ten thousand copies of the *Revolution* were first published on January 8, 1868. Stanton and Anthony's strong stand for women's equal rights was reflected by the masthead of the newspaper: "Principles, not policy: justice, not favors. Men, their rights and nothing more: Women, their rights and nothing less."

In its first few issues, the *Revolution* published a series of articles on women's suffrage. "We shall show that the ballot will secure for woman equal place and equal wages in the world of work; that it will open to her the schools, colleges, professions and all opportunities and advantages of life," the editors wrote. They believed that any other rights a woman won would not be enough until she could also vote.

The *Revolution*'s editors often argued with people who did not agree with them. In the April 23, 1868, issue, they republished an article by a man named Miles O'Reilly. He believed that women should devote their time and energy to taking care of their children rather than fighting for women's suffrage. As he put it, "It is of infinitely more importance that the ladies should have brains and babies than that they should flaunt

The May 26, 1870, issue of the *Revolution* included a report on the work accomplished by the NWSA in its first year.

bonnets and ballots." In response, one of the *Revolution*'s editors offered "to clear up your vision on this question." She refused his categorization of women and explained, "The women who demand the ballot are those who have brains and babies." In other words, she believed there was no conflict between family life and women's rights.

Even though the *Revolution* was popular with working-class women, it did not make a lot of money. By 1870, Anthony had to pay $10,000 of her own money to pay off the debt for the newspaper. The focus of the newspaper changed when Anthony turned it over to Laura Curtis Bullard, who published the paper under the name the *Revolution* until 1872.

WOMAN'S JOURNAL

Like the NWSA, the AWSA had its own newspaper, *Woman's Journal*. Its original editors were Lucy Stone; her husband, Henry Browne Blackwell; and Julia Ward Howe. Much more successful than the *Revolution*, *Woman's Journal* was published from 1870 until 1931. The purpose of the paper was to secure a woman's "educational, industrial, legal and political equality, and especially . . . her right of suffrage."

While women's suffrage still did not have much support outside of the AWSA and NWSA, there was plenty of suffrage news in *Woman's Journal*. In 1886, Senator Henry W. Blair of New Hampshire proposed an amendment for women's suffrage. *Woman's Journal* encouraged all of its readers to write to their senators and representatives in support. Though the measure did not pass, Blair kept trying. A year later, sixteen senators voted in favor of women's suffrage, which was "a great gain," according to *Woman's Journal*. Also in 1887, the

WOMAN'S JOURNAL
AND SUFFRAGE NEWS

VOL. XLIV. NO. 10   SATURDAY, MARCH 8, 1913   FIVE CENTS

PARADE STRUGGLES TO VICTORY DESPITE DISGRACEFUL SCENES

Nation Aroused by Open Insults to Women—Cause Wins Popular Sympathy—Congress Orders Investigation—Striking Object Lesson

Washington has been disgraced. Equal suffrage has scored a great victory. Thousands of indifferent women have been aroused. Influential men are incensed and the United States Senate demands an investigation of the treatment given the suffragists at the National Capital on Monday.

Ten thousand women from all over the country had planned a magnificent parade and pageant to take place in Washington on March 3. Artists, pageant leaders, designers, women of influence and renown were ready to give a wonderful and beautiful piece of suffrage work to the public that would throng the National Capital for the inauguration festivities. The suffragists were ready; the whole procession started down Pennsylvania avenue, when the police protection, that had been promised, failed them, and a disgraceful scene followed. The crowd surged into the space which had been marked off for the paraders, and the leaders of the suffrage movement were compelled to push their way through a mob of the worst element in Washington and vicinity. Women were spit upon, slapped in the face, tripped up, pelted with burning cigar stubs, and insulted by jeers and obscene language too vile to print or repeat.

The cause of all the trouble is apparent when the facts are known. The police authorities in Washington opposed every attempt to have a suffrage parade at all. Having been forbidden a place in the inaugural procession, the suffragists asked to have a procession of their own on March 3. They were finally told that they could have a procession but that it could not be on Pennsylvania avenue, but must be on a side street. At last they got permission to have the suffrage parade on the avenue, and asked that traffic be excluded from the street during the parade. For a long time this was denied, and only on Saturday were they successful.

Everything was at last arranged; it was a glorious day; ten thousand women were ready to do their part to make the parade beautiful to behold to make it a credit to womanhood and to demonstrate the strength of the movement for their enfranchisement.

The police were determined, however, and they had their way. Their attempt to afford the marchers protection and keep the space of the avenue free for the suffrage procession was the flimsiest sham. Police officers stood by with folded arms and grinned while the picked women of the land were insulted and roughly abused by an ignorant and uncouth mob.

Miss Alice Paul and other suffragists were compelled to drive their automobiles down the avenue to separate the crowds as the suffragists with the banners and floats could pass. The police officials say their force was inadequate to handle the crowds, but it is noted that there was no disorder on the avenue during the inaugural procession. It is stated that federal troops were offered to the chief of police for the suffrage procession, but that he refused their aid. At any rate, assistance was finally called from Fort Myer and mounted soldiers drove back the crowd so that the straggling line of marchers could pass through.

Not only were the suffragists bitterly disappointed in having the effect

(Continued on Page 78)

(Continued on Page 78)

AMENDMENT WINS IN NEW JERSEY

Easy Victory in Assembly 46 to 5—Equal Suffrage Enthusiasm Runs High

The New Jersey Legislature passed the woman suffrage amendment in the Assembly last week by a vote of 46 to 5. The Senate had already voted favorably 14 to 5.

A large delegation of suffragists crowded the galleries, and when the overwhelming vote was announced there was a scene of great enthusiasm. Women stood in their seats and waved handkerchiefs and "votes for women" flags and cheered themselves hoarse.

Dr. Jekyll Becomes Mr. Hyde

Opposition was confined exclusively to the old sentimental arguments.

(Continued on Page 79)

(Continued on Page 79)

MICHIGAN AGAIN CAMPAIGN STATE

Senate Passes Suffrage Amendment 26 to 5 and Battle Is Now On

Michigan is again a campaign State after a short lapse of four months. The amendment will go to the voters on April 7. The State-wide feeling that the women were defrauded of victory last fall will help the suffragists.

The final action of the Legislature was taken last week, when the Senate, by a vote of 26 to 5, passed the suffrage amendment, with a slight amendment to make the requirements for foreign-born women the same as those for male immigrants.

Governor Watches Debate

The debate in the Senate lasted an hour and a quarter, and was characterized by the persistent efforts of Senator Weadock and a few others to tack on crippling amendments. Several suggestions, including the disabling of women for holding office or serving on juries, were voted down in quick succession.

Gov. Ferris was among the visitors who crowded the chamber and gallery. Mrs. Clara B. Arthur, Mrs. Thomas R. Henderson and Mrs. Wilbur Brotherton, of Detroit; Mrs. Jennie Law Hardy, of Tecumseh, and other State leaders were present, supported by a large delegation of Lansing suffragists.

The final stand of the opposition was made by Senator Martha in the hope of putting off the submission till November, 1914, and this also failed.

Of the five who opposed the measure on the final roll-call, three were from Detroit.

A complete campaign of organization and education has been mapped out by the State Association. The

(Continued on Page 74.)

(Continued on Page 74.)

General Rosalie Jones in Pilgrim Costume; Miss Inez Milholland on White Steed Leading the Parade; One of the Scores of Imposing Floats; One View of the Procession

On March 8, 1913, *Woman's Journal* reported on the recent suffragist parade in Washington, D.C. The march was interrupted by a mob of people who disapproved of women's suffrage. (For a transcription, see pages 51–52.)

editors were overjoyed to report some small successes. Kansas and New York began to allow women to vote in municipal elections.

Beyond suffrage, *Woman's Journal* reported on women's issues all across the country and even in Europe. It often published letters from readers who shared their experiences. Like in the *Revolution*, the editors would respond to people who believed women belonged in the home and should not fight for equal rights.

THE WEST LEADS THE WAY

On December 10, 1869, the territory of Wyoming became the first place in the United States where women could vote in all elections. Only about seven thousand people lived in Wyoming, and just one thousand of them were women. The legislators hoped that women's suffrage would bring attention to the rural territory and convince more women to move there.

Three months later, Utah Territory also gave women the right to vote. Utah had a much larger population, most of whom were Mormons. In the nineteenth century, the Mormon Church still believed in polygamy, a practice in which a man could have more than one wife. Many Americans did not approve of polygamy. Since Utah was not yet a state, the United States Congress could control more of Utah's government. Congress passed several laws to limit the power of the Mormon polygamists. And because women in

(continued on the next page)

(continued from the previous page)

Utah tended to vote for male polygamists, the congressmen decided that women's suffrage there was promoting polygamy. In 1887, Congress outlawed women's suffrage in Utah.

Women were given voting rights in Washington Territory in 1883, but the territory's supreme court ruled that unconstitutional four years later. For a while Wyoming, which became a state in 1890, was once again the only place where American women could vote. The next state to pass women's suffrage was Colorado, in 1893. When Utah became a state in 1896, it outlawed polygamy and also reapproved women's suffrage.

SUSAN B. ANTHONY'S TRIAL

In the 1870s, the suffragists came up with a different strategy for gaining the vote. They called it the New Departure. Even though part of the Fourteenth Amendment referred only to males, a different section granted citizenship to women. It said, "All persons born and naturalized in the United States . . . are citizens of the United States." Therefore, suffragists argued, women were citizens who had the same rights as men. And if women were equal citizens, then they should have the right to vote.

Using this logic, Susan B. Anthony organized a group of women in 1872 in Rochester, New York, her hometown. They convinced men at the voter registration office to allow them to register. A few days later, Anthony and several other women were able to cast their votes.

Anthony voted for the Republican candidates, including the eventual victor, Ulysses S. Grant, for president.

But less than two weeks later, she was arrested and put on trial for voting illegally. Anthony was found guilty on June 19, 1873. The judge ruled that the Fourteenth Amendment did not give women the right to vote. Anthony was denied an appeal for a new trial by jury and received a notice to pay a fine of $100. She refused to pay the fine, and the government never forced her to do so.

Anthony's attempt to vote in an election gained more attention for the women's suffrage movement. However, many people saw her as a troublemaker and ridiculed her for her beliefs. Public opinion never stopped Anthony from fighting for women's rights. She continued speaking to groups across the country. Many women still were not interested in voting. Anthony hoped

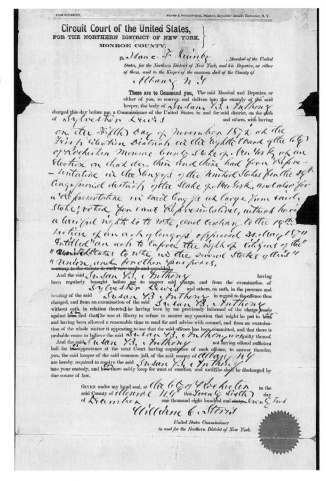

This warrant for Susan B. Anthony's arrest was issued after she voted in the election on November 5, 1872. (For a transcription, see pages 52–53.)

to persuade them that voting was important and worth fighting for.

Other women tried to use Anthony's argument that women had the right of suffrage because they were citizens of the United States. Virginia Minor also attempted to register to vote in 1872. She sued the voting registrar, Reese Happersett, when he would not take her application. The case went to the Supreme Court of the United States in 1875. Unfortunately, the court ruled against Minor. All the justices agreed that she was a citizen, but they did not think that all citizens had the right to vote under the Fourteenth Amendment.

Minor v. Happersett was a blow to Stanton, Anthony, and the NWSA. They had tried to argue that the Constitution indirectly gave women the right to vote. Now they had lost. Women would have to gain suffrage in individual states, which was the AWSA's strategy.

GETTING THE WORD OUT

Stanton and Anthony traveled extensively during the 1870s and 1880s. They gave speeches and held meetings to educate women about the need for a national suffrage amendment. They spoke in small frontier towns and in big cities, anywhere they could find someone to listen. Traveling provided opportunities for Stanton and Anthony to meet many women's rights supporters at the local and state levels. They participated in individual state campaigns for suffrage. Anthony addressed legislatures and congressional committees hoping to gain political support for a woman's suffrage amendment.

Anthony gave a speech called "Social Purity" in a Sunday afternoon Dime lecture course on March 14, 1875, at the Grand Opera House in Chicago. She spoke to

DECLARATION OF RIGHTS

OF THE

WOMEN OF THE UNITED STATES

BY THE

NATIONAL WOMAN SUFFRAGE ASSOCIATION,

JULY 4th, 1876.

WHILE the Nation is buoyant with patriotism, and all hearts are attuned to praise, it is with sorrow we come to strike the one discordant note, on this hundredth anniversary of our country's birth. When subjects of Kings, Emperors, and Czars, from the Old World, join in our National Jubilee, shall the women of the Republic refuse to lay their hands with benedictions on the nation's head? Surveying America's Exposition, surpassing in magnificence those of London, Paris, and Vienna, shall we not rejoice at the success of the youngest rival among the nations of the earth? May not our hearts, in unison with all, swell with pride at our great achievements as a people; our free speech, free press, free schools, free church, and the rapid progress we have made in material wealth, trade, commerce, and the inventive arts? And we do rejoice, in the success thus far, of our experiment of self-government. Our faith is firm and unwavering in the broad principles of human rights, proclaimed in 1776, not only as abstract truths, but as the corner stones of a republic. Yet, we cannot forget, even in this glad hour, that while all men of every race, and clime, and condition, have been invested with the full rights of citizenship, under our hospitable flag, all women still suffer the degradation of disfranchisement.

The history of our country the past hundred years, has been a series of assumptions and usurpations of power over woman, in direct opposition to the principles of just government, acknowledged by the United States at its foundation, which are:

First. The natural rights of each individual.

Second. The exact equality of these rights.

Third. That these rights, when not delegated by the individual, are retained by the individual.

Fourth. That no person can exercise the rights of others without delegated authority.

Fifth. That the non-use of these rights does not destroy them.

And for the violation of these fundamental principles of our Government, we arraign our rulers on this 4th day of July, 1876,—and these are our

ARTICLES OF IMPEACHMENT.

BILLS OF ATTAINDER have been passed by the introduction of the word "male" into all the State constitutions, denying to woman the right of suffrage, and thereby making sex a crime—an exercise of power clearly forbidden in Article 1st, Sections 9th and 10th of the United States Constitution.

On the one-hundredth anniversary of the United States, the NWSA issued the Declaration of Rights of the Women of the United States. It protested that women had still not been given equal rights, especially the right to vote. (For a transcription, please see pages 53–54.)

a large crowd about the social problems of the time and how they affected women. Anthony emphasized that in order for women to make lasting changes in society, they must be given the right to vote and the opportunity to share an equal voice in making decisions at all levels of the government. Because of Anthony's persuasive speaking style, her lectures convinced many people to support women's suffrage.

In 1876, Anthony and Stanton wrote a Declaration of Rights for Women. They took it to the Fourth of July ceremonies at the Centennial Exposition in Philadelphia. After being denied permission to read it formally, they handed out copies to members of the crowd. Anthony later read the declaration to a large group that had formed outside to hear her speak.

In 1877, Anthony collected petitions from twenty-six states—totaling ten thousand signatures—and asked Congress to consider passing an amendment for women's suffrage, but Congress did not acknowledge them. However, Anthony and Stanton did see some progress as the result of many years of hard work. By the late 1800s, women had won the right to vote in school board and local elections in several states. In 1878, Anthony wrote a federal suffrage amendment that was introduced in every congress until women were granted the right to vote in 1920.

CHAPTER FIVE

VICTORY AT LAST

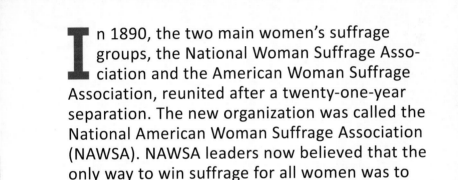

In 1890, the two main women's suffrage groups, the National Woman Suffrage Association and the American Woman Suffrage Association, reunited after a twenty-one-year separation. The new organization was called the National American Woman Suffrage Association (NAWSA). NAWSA leaders now believed that the only way to win suffrage for all women was to work at gaining it one state at a time. It was clear that there was not enough support for women's suffrage in Congress. But if the majority of the states let women vote, then Congress would have to pass a constitutional amendment granting women's suffrage throughout the United States.

"THE SOLITUDE OF SELF"

In January 1892, Elizabeth Cady Stanton and other NAWSA members met with the House Judiciary Committee to ask for a women's suffrage amendment. Stanton read a speech she had written called "The Solitude of Self." She discussed why it was important for women to be recognized as individuals, saying:

The strongest reason why we ask for woman a voice in the government under which she lives; in the religion she is asked to believe; equality in social life, where she is the chief factor; a place in the trades and professions, where she may earn her bread is because, as an individual, she must rely on herself . . . Who, I ask you, can take, dare take, on himself the rights, the duties, the responsibilities of another human soul?

The Woman's Bible was very controversial when it was released. In this draft, Stanton discussed the parable of Balaam in the Book of Numbers.

Stanton talked about the fact that a woman, just like any other person, was responsible for herself and her actions. Doing that for oneself was hard enough, she reasoned. It would be impossible for men to also represent the views of all women. That was why it was so crucial for women to have their own rights and the ability to express their opinions publicly.

Stanton and others believed this was the best speech she had ever written. Anthony said that Stanton's speech was "the strongest and most unanswerable argument and appeal ever made

. . . for the full freedom and franchise of women." The speech was published as a book later that year.

However, some of Stanton's views were considered very radical. She published *The Woman's Bible, Part 1* in 1895. This book was Stanton's view on how the Bible influenced women's roles in society. She felt that many teachings in the Bible discriminated against women and kept them from working together as equals with men. Stanton's interpretation of the Bible shocked and angered many women's rights activists, as well as people opposed to women's suffrage. NAWSA made a public statement clarifying that this was Stanton's personal opinion, not the opinion of NAWSA as a whole. *The Woman's Bible*, unlike so many of Stanton's other articles and speeches, was never universally accepted.

NEW LEADERS TAKE THE TORCH

From the late 1890s through 1910, NAWSA went through some major changes as new leaders of the women's movement became involved. The two most important leaders, Stanton and Anthony, had fought for half a century to gain women's rights, but they did not live to see women gain the right to vote. Stanton passed away in 1902, and Anthony died in 1906.

Carrie Chapman Catt joined NAWSA in 1890 and worked actively to gain state-by-state suffrage. In 1894, Catt led the successful suffrage campaign in Colorado. By 1896, Wyoming, Colorado, Utah, and Idaho had gained full suffrage. Catt's enthusiasm and organizational skills strengthened NAWSA, inspired supporters, and brought in new members. She took over as president of NAWSA when Anthony resigned in 1900. In 1904, Catt resigned her position but remained active in the organization.

KAISER WILSON

HAVE YOU FORGOTTEN YOUR SYMPATHY WITH THE POOR GERMANS BECAUSE THEY WERE NOT SELF-GOVERNED?

20,000,000 AMERICAN WOMEN ARE NOT SELF-GOVERNED.

TAKE THE BEAM OUT OF YOUR OWN EYE.

Alice Paul was arrested for picketing the White House in 1917. She compared President Wilson to Kaiser Wilhelm of Germany, the United States' opponent in World War I.

Harriot Stanton Blatch, Stanton's daughter, worked hard to bring a new suffrage bill to both houses of the New York State legislature for debate. Blatch formed the Equality League of Self-Supporting Women in 1907, which became known as the Women's Political Union in 1910. She actively organized campaigns, speakers, and pickets in order to gain attention for women's suffrage.

Blatch's approach attracted many middle-class women who were new to the women's suffrage movement. Blatch organized open-air meetings and a large parade in which suffragists marched down Fifth Avenue in New York City on May 21, 1910. This parade was the first of many demonstrations organized to draw attention to women's suffrage. By 1916, the Women's Political Union merged with the Congressional Union, later known as the National Woman's Party. Alice Paul was its leader.

SLOW AND STEADY WINS THE RACE

In the second decade of the twentieth century, the suffrage movement in individual states gained momentum. Again, states in the western part of the country led the way. Between 1910 and 1914, Washington, California, Oregon, Kansas, Arizona, Alaska, Montana, and Nevada passed full women's suffrage. New York in 1917 became the first state east of the Mississippi River to allow women to vote in all elections.

Other states changed their voting laws to give women a limited form of suffrage. Sometimes women were allowed to vote only in presidential elections. Other states said they could vote only in local elections or for members of the school board.

By 1915, many western states had allowed women's suffrage. This map shows Lady Liberty moving toward the eastern states that did not let women vote yet.

Another major victory came in 1916. Jeannette Rankin was elected to the U.S. House of Representatives as a Republican from Montana. She famously declared, "I may be the first woman member of Congress. But I won't be the last." As a congresswoman, she voted against the United States entering World War I. NAWSA worried that her stance would make the suffragists look bad. Yet Rankin also helped the suffragist cause by calling for Congress to create a committee on women's suffrage. She was appointed to the new committee and argued persuasively for women's suffrage.

ALICE PAUL'S PROTESTS

Alice Paul of the National Woman's Party had more radical ideas about how to gain attention for women's suffrage. She participated in the suffrage movement in England. Suffragists there were sometimes arrested for their violent protests. In prison, they went on hunger strikes. Guards sometimes forced them to eat, which was very painful.

Back in the United States, Paul organized a suffragist march on Washington, D.C., that drew a large crowd of suffragists in

Suffragists had wanted to march in the inaugural parade on March 4, 1913. When they were denied, they planned a separate march for the day before.

1913. It was held the day before Woodrow Wilson's presidential inauguration. The suffragists hoped to gain more public support for their cause. Instead, many opponents of women's suffrage showed up and formed a mob. Army troops were later sent in to control the angry crowd.

Tension within the movement continued to build as supporters grew impatient at the lack of progress. Carrie Chapman Catt was reelected as the NAWSA president in 1915. This time she decided to work two different strategies at the same time. While continuing to push suffrage efforts in separate states, NAWSA also began lobbying for women's suffrage on the national level. A new constitutional amendment giving all women the right to vote would be the Nineteenth Amendment.

Paul believed that with President Wilson's support, the amendment would pass in Congress. She and her supporters in the National Woman's Party continued a series of protests that included picketing the White House. Like the English suffragists, they also went on hunger strikes.

President Wilson finally agreed to support women's suffrage publicly in 1918. World War I was one of the reasons he changed his opinion. Women were taking on new jobs as men went to Europe to help the Allies defeat the Central Powers. This helped some people realize that women were capable and deserved to have a say in political matters.

THE NINETEENTH AMENDMENT AND BEYOND

Finally, on June 4, 1919, both the House of Representatives and the Senate agreed to pass the Nineteenth Amendment, also known as the Susan B. Anthony Amendment. Suffragists

Women voted in New York for the first time in 1917. Three years later, women could vote all across the country.

immediately went to work on getting the amendment ratified by the required thirty-six states. Their final campaign lasted another fourteen months. In anticipation of the amendment's approval, NAWSA voted in February 1920 to change its name to the League of Women Voters.

On August 18, 1920, after a long, hard battle, the Nineteenth Amendment to the Constitution was adopted, more than seventy-two years after the Seneca Falls Convention. Women across the country finally had the right to vote in all elections!

Winning suffrage was not the end of the women's rights movement, however. Women could now express their

THE EQUAL RIGHTS AMENDMENT

Alice Paul believed the Nineteenth Amendment would not end discrimination against women. She proposed another constitutional amendment: "Men and women shall have equal rights throughout the United States." This became known as the Equal Rights Amendment, or ERA. It was first introduced in Congress in 1923. Almost fifty years later, in 1973, the ERA finally passed Congress. Some states ratified it, but there was a deadline for getting three-fourths of the states to approve it. Not enough states passed the ERA in time.

opinion through voting, but they were still not treated equally, especially in the workplace. The Civil Rights Act of 1964 made it illegal to discriminate against people because of their race, religion, national origin, or sex. Unlike the amendments passed during Reconstruction one hundred years earlier, this important law protected women alongside African Americans and other minorities.

Still, women are not treated equal to men in all ways, even a century after the Nineteenth Amendment. Women earn less money than men on average and are less likely to be chief executives of businesses or members of Congress. But progress is being made every day. For example, a record 104 women are in the 114th Congress. Just like Susan B. Anthony, Elizabeth Cady Stanton, and the rest of the suffragists, women today continue to fight for equal rights.

TIMELINE

March 31, 1776: Abigail Adams writes a letter to her husband, President John Adams, asking that he "remember the Ladies" when helping to write the U.S. Constitution.

1833: Lucretia Mott is elected president of the Philadelphia Female Anti-Slavery Society.

June 20, 1840: Women delegates are prevented from participating at the World Anti-Slavery Convention in London.

July 19–20, 1848: The first women's rights convention takes place in Seneca Falls, New York.

1851: Sojourner Truth gives a speech called "Ain't I a Woman?" at the Woman's Rights Convention in Akron, Ohio.
Elizabeth Cady Stanton and Susan B. Anthony meet for the first time and begin their fifty-year partnership working for women's rights and suffrage.

December 6, 1865: The Thirteenth Amendment is ratified, abolishing slavery in the United States.

May 10, 1866: The American Equal Rights Association is founded by Anthony, Stanton, Mott, and Lucy Stone.

July 28, 1868: The Fourteenth Amendment is ratified, granting equal protection under the law to all citizens (including former slaves). It also uses the word "male" to refer to eligible voters.

May 1869: The women's rights movement splits into two groups: the National Woman Suffrage Association (NWSA) and the American Woman Suffrage Association (AWSA).

December 10, 1869: The territory of Wyoming is the first U.S. territory or state to grant unlimited suffrage to women.

February 3, 1870: The Fifteenth Amendment is ratified, giving black men the right to vote.

November 5, 1872: Anthony is arrested for attempting to vote in a presidential election.

1890: The NWSA and the AWSA merge to form the National American Woman Suffrage Association (NAWSA).

March 3, 1913: More than five thousand women attend a women's suffrage march in Washington, D.C., organized by Alice Paul.

June 4, 1919: Congress passes the Nineteenth Amendment, and suffragists begin their state-by-state ratification campaign.

February 14, 1920: The name of NAWSA is changed to the League of Women Voters.

August 18, 1920: The Nineteenth Amendment is ratified, allowing women in the United States the unlimited right to vote.

PAGE 25: "A PETITION FOR UNIVERSAL SUFFRAGE," C. 1865

To the Senate and House of Representatives:

The undersigned, Women of the United States, respectfully ask an amendment of the Constitution that shall prohibit the several States from disenfranchising any of their citizens on the ground of sex.

In making our demand for Suffrage, we would call your attention to the fact that we represent fifteen million people—one half of the entire population of the country—intelligent, virtuous, native-born Americans citizens; and yet stand outside the pole of political recognition.

The Constitution classes us as "free people," and counts us *whole* persons in the basis of representation and yet are we governed without our consent, compelled to pay taxes without appeal, and punished for violations of law without choice of judge or juror.

The experience of all ages, the Declarations of the Fathers, the Statute Laws of our day, and the fearful revolution through which we have just passed, all prove the uncertain tenure of life, liberty and property so long as the ballot—the only weapon of self-protection—is not in the hand of every citizen.

Therefore, as you are now amending the Constitution, and, in harmony with advancing civilization, placing new safeguards round the individual rights of four millions of emancipated slaves, we ask that you extend the right of Suffrage to Woman—the only remaining class of disenfranchised citizens—and thus fulfil your Constitutional obligation "to Guarantee to every State in the Union a Republican form of Government."

As all partial application of Republican principles must ever breed a complicated legislation as well as a discontented people, we would pray your Honorable Body, in order to simplify the machinery of government and ensure domestic tranquillity, that you legislate hereafter for persons, citizens, tax-payers, and not for class or caste.

For justice and equality your petitioners will ever pray.

NAMES	RESIDENCE
E Cady Stanton	New York
Susan B. Anthony	Rochester – N.Y.
Antoinette Brown Blackwell	New York
Lucy Stone	Newark N. Jersey
Joanna S. Morse	48 Livingston. Brooklyn
Ernestine B. Rose	New York

Harriet E. Eaton	6. West 14th Street NY
Catharine G. Wilkeson	83 Clinton Place New York
Elizabeth R. Tilton	48 Livingstone St. Brooklyn
Mary Fowler Gilbert	293 W. 19th St New York
Mary S. Gilbert	New York
M Griffith	New York

PAGE 32: EXCERPT FROM "PARADE STRUGGLES TO VICTORY DESPITE DISGRACEFUL SCENES," *WOMAN'S JOURNAL*, MARCH 8, 1913

Washington has been disgraced. Equal suffrage has scored a great victory. Thousands of indifferent women have been aroused. Influential men are incensed and the United States Senate demands an investigation of the treatment given the suffragists at the National Capital on Monday.

Ten thousand women from all over the country had planned a magnificent parade and pageant to take place in Washington on March 3. Artists, pageant leaders, designers, women of influence and renown were ready to give a wonderful and beautiful piece of suffrage work to the public that would throng the National Capital for the inauguration festivities. The suffragists were ready: the whole procession started down Pennsylvania avenue, when the police protection that had been promised, failed them, and a disgraceful scene followed. The crowd surged into the space which had been marked off for the paraders, and the leaders of the suffrage movement were compelled to push their way through a mob of the worst element in Washington and vicinity. Women were spit upon, slapped in the face, tripped up, pelted with burning cigar stubs, and insulted by jeers and obscene language too vile to print or repeat.

The cause of all the trouble is apparent when the facts are known. The police authorities in Washington opposed every attempt to have a suffrage parade at all. Having been forbidden a place in the inaugural procession, the suffragists asked to have a procession of their own on March 3. They were finally told that they could have a procession but that it could not be on Pennsylvania avenue but must be on a side street. At last they got permission to have the suffrage parade on the avenue, and asked that traffic be excluded from the street during the parade. For a long time this was denied, and only on Saturday were they successful.

Everything was at last arranged; it was a glorious day: ten thousand women were ready to do their part to make the parade beautiful to behold, to make it a credit to womanhood and to demonstrate the strength of the movement for their enfranchisement.

The police were determined, however, and they had their way. Their attempt to afford the marchers protection and keep the space of avenue free for the suffrage procession was the flimsiest sham. Police officers stood by with folded arms and grinned while the picked women of the land were insulted and roughly abused by an ignorant and uncouth mob.

Miss Alice Paul and other suffragists were compelled to drive their automobiles down the avenue to separate the crowds so the suffragists with the banners and floats could pass. The police officials say their force was inadequate to handle the crowds, but it is noted that there was no disorder on the avenue during the inaugural procession. It is stated that federal troops were offered to the chief of police for the suffrage procession, but that he refused their aid.

At any rate, assistance was finally called from Fort Myer and mounted soldiers drove back the crowd so that the straggling line of marchers could pass through. ...

PAGE 35: WARRANT FOR SUSAN B. ANTHONY'S ARREST, BY WILLIAM C. STORRS, DECEMBER 26, 1872

Circuit Court of the United States, for the Northern District of New York, Monroe County

To Isaac F. Quinby, Marshal of the United States, for the Northern District of New York, and his Deputies, or either of them, and to the Keeper of the common Jail of the County of Albany NY

These are to Command you, The said Marshal and Deputies, or either of you, to convey and deliver into the custody of the said keeper, the body of Susan B. Anthony charged this day before me, a Commissioner of the United States, in and for said district, on the oath of Sylvester Lewis and others, with having on the Fifth Day of November 1872 on the First Election District in the Eighth Ward of the City of Rochester Monroe County State of New York at an Election on that day then and there had for a Representative in the Congress of the United States for the 29th Congressional district of the State of New York, and also for a Representative in said Congress at large from said state; voted for said Representatives, without having a lawful right so to vote, and contrary to the 19th section of an act of Congress approved 31 May 1870 Entitled "An act to Enforce the right of Citizens of the United States to vote in the several States of this Union, and for other purposes."

And the said Susan B. Anthony having been regularly brought before me to answer said charge, and from the examination of Sylvester Lewis and others, on oath, in the presence and hearing of the said Susan B. Anthony in regard to the offence thus charged, and from an examination of the said Susan B. Anthony, without oath, in relation thereto, she having been by me previously informed of the charge made against her, and that she was at liberty to refuse to answer any question that might be put to her, and having been allowed a reasonable time to send for and advise with counsel, and from an examination of the whole matter it appearing to me that the said offense has been committed, and that there is probable cause to believe the said Susan B. Anthony was guilty thereof.

And the said Susan B. Anthony not having offered sufficient bail for her appearance at the next Court having cognizance of such offence, to answer therefor, you, the said keeper of the said common jail, of the said county of Albany NY are hereby required to receive the said Susan B. Anthony into your custody, and her there safely keep for want of sureties, and until she shall be discharged by due course of law.

Given under my hand seal, at the City of Rochester in the said County of Monroe NY this Twenty Sixth day of December one thousand eight hundred and seventy two

William C. Storrs
United States Commissioner in and for the Northern District of New York

PAGE 37: EXCERPT FROM "DECLARATION OF RIGHTS OF THE WOMEN OF THE UNITED STATES," BY THE NATIONAL WOMAN SUFFRAGE ASSOCIATION, JULY 4, 1876

While the Nation is buoyant with patriotism, and all hearts are attuned to praise, it is with sorrow we come to strike the one discordant note, on this hundredth anniversary of our country's birth. When subjects of Kings, Emperors, and Czars, from the Old World, join in our National Jubilee, shall the women of the Republic refuse to lay their hands with benedictions on the nation's head? Surveying America's Exposition, surpassing in magnificence those of London, Paris, and Vienna, shall we not rejoice at the success of the youngest rival among the nations of the earth? May not our hearts, in unison with all, swell with pride at our great achievements as a people; our free speech, free press, free schools, free church, and the rapid progress we have made in material wealth, trade, commerce, and the inventive arts? And we do rejoice, in the success thus far, of our experiment of self-government. Our faith is firm and unwavering in the broad principles of human rights, proclaimed in 1776, not only as abstract truths, but as the corner stones of a republic. Yet, we cannot forget, even in this glad hour, that while all men of every race, and clime, and condition, have been invested with the full rights of citizenship, under our hospitable flag, all women still suffer the degradation of disenfranchisement.

The history of our country the past hundred years, has been a series of assumptions and usurpations of power over women, in direct opposition to the principles of just government, acknowledged by the United States at its foundation, which are:

First. The natural rights of each individual.

Second. The exact equality of these rights.

Third. That these rights, when not delegated by the individual, are retained by the individual.

Fourth. That no person can exercise the rights of others without delegated authority.

Fifth. That the non-use of these rights does not destroy them.

And for the violation of these fundamental principles of our Government, we arraign our rulers on this 4th date of July, 1876—and these are our

ARTICLES OF IMPEACHMENT.

BILLS OF ATTAINDER have been passed by the introduction of the word "male" into all the State constitutions, denying to woman the right of suffrage, and thereby making sex a crime—an exercise of power clearly forbidden in Article 1st, Sections 9th and 10th of the United States Constitution...

GLOSSARY

abolitionist A person in the nineteenth century who fought to end slavery.

amendment A proposal that changes or makes an addition to a bill, law, or constitution.

citizen A resident of a country who has the rights and protection of that country's government.

constitution A document in which the basic laws and principles of a government are written down.

convention A meeting of members or representatives of a political, social, professional, or religious group.

declaration A formal statement.

democracy A government in which the people have a say, usually by being able to vote for the members who will represent them in government.

discriminate To treat or judge someone unfairly or take away his or her rights because of the person's race, class, or sex.

enfranchise To give someone or a group of people the right to vote.

grievance A formal complaint.

inauguration An event in which the U.S. president is sworn into office at the beginning of his term.

lobby To try to persuade lawmakers to vote for or against an issue.

Quaker A member of the Religious Society of Friends, which is a religious movement known for allowing women to speak at meetings and for being opposed to slavery.

ratify To approve, as an amendment to the Constitution.

referendum A proposal that the public can vote on to decide whether it becomes law.

resolution A formal statement of opinion that is adopted by a group.

sentiment An expression of feelings or opinions as a basis for taking a specific action.

social reform Any movement that works to improve social or political conditions for disadvantaged people, such as women or African Americans.

suffrage The right to vote.

unconstitutional Describing a law that goes against the constitution of a state or country.

FOR MORE INFORMATION

League of Women Voters
1730 M Street NW, Suite 1000
Washington, DC 20036-4508
(202) 429-1965
Website: http://www.lwv.org
The League of Women Voters was founded in 1920, the
    year that women earned the right to vote in the United
    States, as a successor to the National American Woman
    Suffrage Association. Today, it continues to fight for
    expanded public participation in government.

National Organization for Women (NOW)
1100 H Street NW, Suite 300
Washington, DC 20005
(202) 628-8669
Website: http://www.now.org
NOW was founded in 1966 because there was still gender
    inequality, even though the Civil Rights Act of 1964
    had outlawed discrimination against women. The
    organization campaigns for an amendment to the U.S.
    Constitution that would guarantee equal economic and
    political rights for women.

Susan B. Anthony House
17 Madison Street
Rochester, New York 14608
(585) 235-6124
Website: http://www.susanbanthonyhouse.org
The Susan B. Anthony House has been a memorial to
    the legendary women's rights leaders since 1945. By
    sharing Anthony's legacy, the museum and its programs
    aim to inspire visitors to make a difference in their own
    communities.

UN Women
220 East 42nd Street
New York, NY 10017
(646) 781-4400
Website: http://www.unwomen.org/en
UN Women is the United Nations organization that promotes
gender equality and women's empowerment. The
organization's many goals include increasing women's
political participation, both as voters and as leaders,
around the world.

Women's Rights National Historic Park
136 Fall Street
Seneca Falls, NY 13148
(315) 568-0024
Website: http://www.nps.gov/wori/index.htm
This national park in Seneca Falls, New York, celebrates the
first women's rights convention, held there in 1848.
Visitors can also tour Wesleyan Chapel, which hosted
the convention; the house where Elizabeth Cady Stanton
lived from 1847 until 1862; and M'Clintock House, where
the Declaration of Sentiments was drafted.

WEBSITES

Because of the changing nature of Internet links, Rosen
Publishing has developed an online list of websites related
to the subject of this book. This site is updated regularly.
Please use this link to access the list:

http://www.rosenlinks.com/UAH/Women

FOR FURTHER READING

Benoit, Peter. *Women's Right to Vote* (Cornerstones of Freedom). New York, NY: Scholastic Children's Press, 2014.

Carson, Mary Kay. *Why Couldn't Susan B. Anthony Vote? And Other Questions About Women's Suffrage* (Good Question!). New York, NY: Sterling Children's Books, 2015.

Colman, Penny. *Elizabeth Cady Stanton and Susan B. Anthony: A Friendship That Changed the World*. New York, NY: Henry Holt and Company, 2011.

Gelletly, LeeAnne. *Seeking the Right to Vote* (Finding a Voice: Women's Fight for Equality in U.S. Society). Broomall, PA: Mason Crest, 2013.

Gullain, Charlotte. *Stories of Women's Suffrage: Votes for Women!* (Women's Stories from History). Portsmouth, NH: Heinemann, 2015.

Hollihan, Kerrie Logan. *Rightfully Ours: How Women Won the Vote*. Chicago, IL: Chicago Review Press, 2012.

Lusted, Marcia Amidon. *The Fight for Women's Suffrage* (Essential Events). Edina, MN: ABDO Publishing Company, 2011.

Metz, Lorijo. *The Women's Suffrage Movement* (Let's Celebrate Freedom!). New York, NY: PowerKids Press, 2014.

Orr, Tamra. *A History of Voting Rights in America* (Vote America). Hockessin, DE: Mitchell Lane, 2012.

Penn, Barbra. *Susan B. Anthony* (Britannica Beginner Bios). New York, NY: Britannica Educational Publishing, 2015.

Shea, Nicole. *Elizabeth Cady Stanton in Her Own Words* (Eyewitness to History). New York, NY: Gareth Stevens Publishing, 2014.

Yousafzai, Malala. *I Am Malala: How One Girl Stood Up for Education and Changed the World* (Young Readers Edition). New York, NY: Little, Brown Books for Young Readers, 2014.

BIBLIOGRAPHY

Adams, Abigail. "Letter from Abigail Adams to John Adams, 31 March–5 April 1776." Adams Family Papers: An Electronic Archive, Massachusetts Historical Society. Retrieved November 7, 2014 (http://www.masshist.org /digitaladams).

Dudden, Faye E. *Fighting Chance: The Struggle over Woman Suffrage and Black Suffrage in Reconstruction America*. New York, NY: Oxford University Press, 2011.

Library of Congress. American Treasures of the Library of Congress. "The Seneca Falls Convention." Retrieved November 5, 2014 (http://www.loc.gov/exhibits /treasures/trr040.html).

Linder, Doug. "The Trial of Susan B. Anthony for Illegal Voting." University of Missouri-Kansas City School of Law. Retrieved November 5, 2014 (http://law2.umkc .edu/faculty/projects/ftrials/anthony/sbaaccount.html).

New York Times. "Elizabeth Cady Stanton Dies at Her Home." October 27, 1902. Retrieved November 5, 2014 (http://www.nytimes.com/learning/general/onthisday/ bday/1112.html).

PBS. *Not for Ourselves Alone: The Story of Elizabeth Cady Stanton and Susan B. Anthony*. "Seneca Falls Convention." Retrieved November 6, 2014 (http:// www.pbs.org/stantonanthony/resources/index .html?body=seneca_falls.html).

Rea, Tom. "Right Choice, Wrong Reasons: Wyoming Women Win the Right to Vote." Wyoming State Historical Society. Retrieved November 5, 2014 (http://www.wyohistory.org/essays/right-choice -wrong-reasons-wyoming-women-win-right-vote).

Stanton, Elizabeth Cady. "Address by Elizabeth Cady Stanton on Woman's Rights in 1848." The Elizabeth Cady Stanton and Susan B. Anthony Papers Project,

Rutgers University. Retrieved November 5, 2014
(http://ecssba.rutgers.edu/docs/ecswoman1.html).

Stanton, Elizabeth Cady. "Solitude of Self." *Not for
Ourselves Alone: The Story of Elizabeth Cady Stanton
and Susan B. Anthony* (PBS). Retrieved November
6, 2014 (http://www.pbs.org/stantonanthony/
resources/index.html?body=solitude_self.html).

Susan B. Anthony Center for Women's Leadership.
"Suffrage History." University of Rochester.
Retrieved November 5, 2014 (http://www.rochester
.edu/sba/suffragehistory/index.html).

Susan B. Anthony Center for Women's Leadership. "US
Suffrage Movement Timeline, 1792 to Present." University
of Rochester. Retrieved November 5, 2014 (http://www
.rochester.edu/sba/suffragehistory/timeline.html).

United States House of Representatives: History, Art & Archives.
"Rankin, Jeannette." Retrieved November 5, 2014 (http://
history.house.gov/People/Listing/R/RANKIN,-Jeannette
-(R000055)/).

Wagner, Sally Roesch. "The Untold Story of the Iroquois
Influence on Early Feminists." *On the Issues*, Winter 1996.
Retrieved November 5, 2014 (http://www.feminist.com
/resources/artspeech/genwom/iroquoisinfluence.html).

Washington Secretary of State. "Voting Rights for Women,
Women's Suffrage." Retrieved November 5, 2014 (https://
sos.wa.gov/elections/timeline/suffrage.htm).

Weatherford, Doris. *A History of the American Suffragist
Movement*. New York, NY: MTM Publishing, 2005.

INDEX

ABOUT THE AUTHORS

Meredith Day is an editor and writer from Connecticut. She graduated with a bachelor of arts in history from Colgate University. Her senior thesis centered on Mormon women's suffrage in Utah, which in 1870 became the second U.S. territory to give women the vote.

Colleen Adams is an editor and writer of children's books. She lives in Lockport, New York, with her husband and two children.

PHOTO CREDITS

Designer: Michael Moy; Editor: Meredith Day